KT-468-850

Time to eat.
Who's hungry?

Crunch, crunch! Yum!

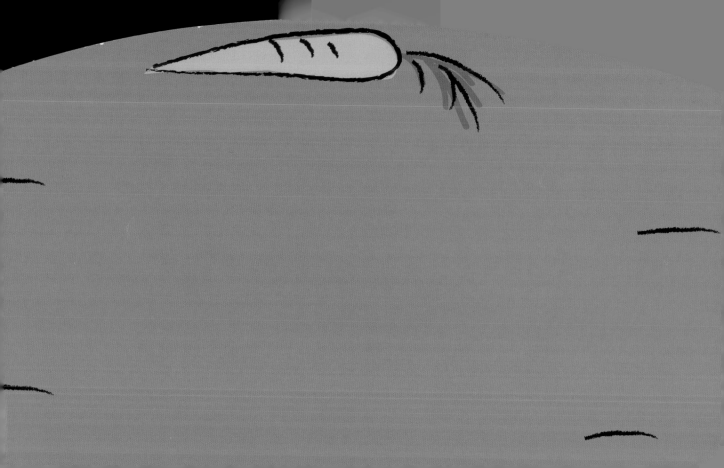

Glad you like it, Bunny.
Who else is hungry?

I am! I would love
a fresh fish, please.

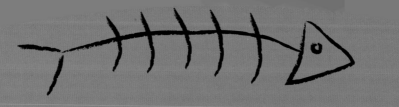

Slurp! Gulp! Delicious!

You're quick, Seal!
Who else is hungry?

I am! Bananas are
my favourite.

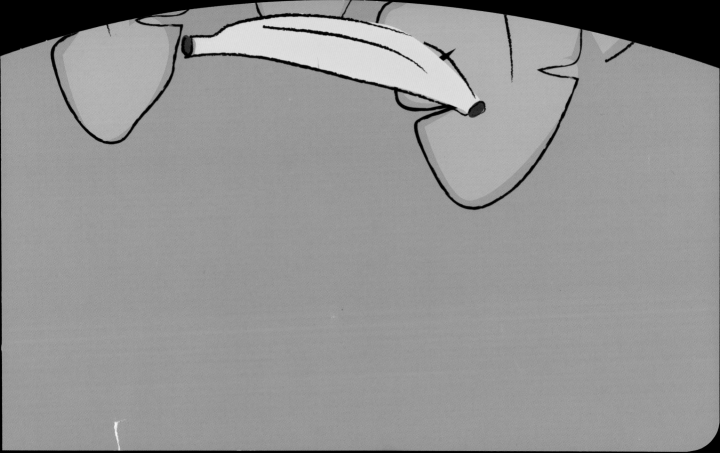

Mmmm! Thank you.

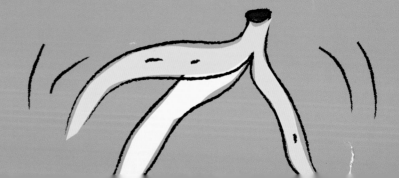

You're welcome, Monkey.
Who else is hungry?

I am!
I like hay.

What a big appetite, Horse!
Who else is hungry?

I am! I would like an acorn, please.

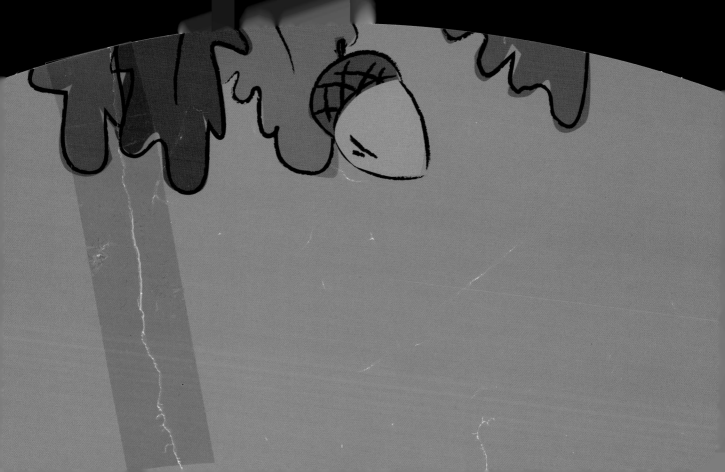

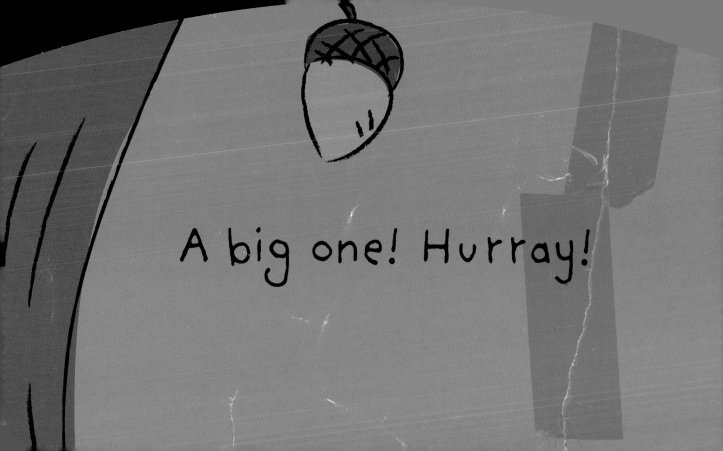

It's all yours, Squirrel.
Who else is hungry?

I am! I can't wait
to chew some bamboo.

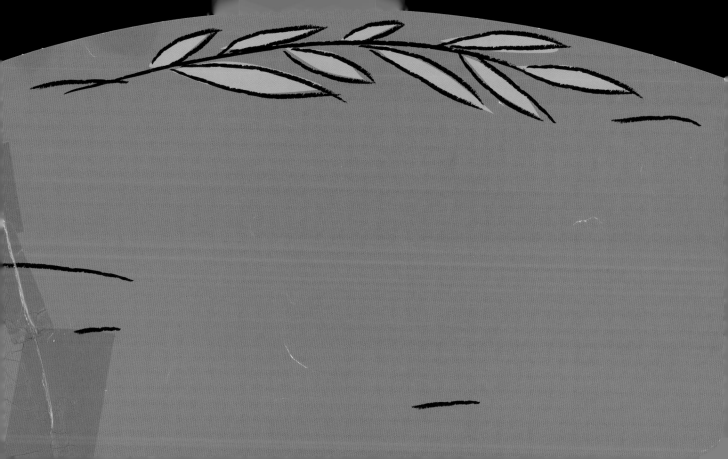

There's plenty more, Panda!
Who else is hungry?

I am! Please may I have some cheese?

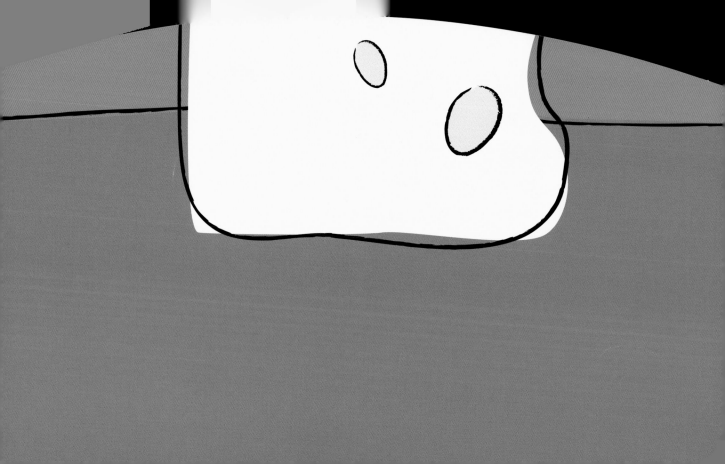

So tasty!

Enjoy it, Mouse!
Is anyone else hungry?

Are you hungry?
Eat up!